THE SLEEPING BEAUTY

19 잠자는 숲 속의 미녀

Charles Perrault

Adapted by **Lori Olcott**
Illustrated by **Hong Hee-Kyoung**

Copyright © WORLDCOM 2003

Published in Korea in 2003 by WORLDCOM

All rights reserved. No part of this publication may be reproduced, stored in a retrieval system, or transmitted in any form or by any means, electronic, mechanical, photocopying, recording, or otherwise, without the prior written permission of the publisher.

Printed and distributed by WORLDCOM

작가와 작품 설명

샤를 페로(Charles Perrault)는 프랑스 파리 태생의 동화작가이다. 17세기 프랑스를 대표하는 비평가이기도 한 그는 1670년 아카데미 프랑세즈 회원이 되어 집회에서 낭독한 『루이 대왕의 세기(世紀)』를 계기로 커다란 논쟁을 불러 일으키기도 했다. 그가 쓴 동화의 제재(題材)로는 후세의 『그림 동화』와 공통된 것이 많으나, 현실과 상상의 세계가 절묘하게 조화되어, 그를 프랑스 아동문학의 아버지라고 부르기도 한다.

그는 『잠자는 숲 속의 미녀』 외에도 유럽의 민담에 문학적 표현을 가미한 『푸른 수염』, 『빨간 망토』, 『신데렐라』, 『장화신은 고양이』 등 교훈적인 내용의 동화를 많이 썼다.

작품 설명

오로라 공주는 그녀의 세례식에 초대받지 못한 심술궂은 요정으로부터 물레에 손가락이 찔려 죽을 것이라는 무서운 저주를 받는다. 다행히도 선한 요정이 이 저주를 100년 간의 잠으로 바꾸어 준다. 공주를 보호하려는 왕과 왕비의 노력에도 불구하고 어느날 공주는 물레에 손가락을 찔려 성과 더불어 잠들게 된다. 가시덩쿨로 둘러싸인 성에는 아무도 접근할 수 없는데…. 과연 오로라 공주는 깨어날 수 있을까?

Introduction

Hello, and thank you for your interest in Worldcom's Story House! I hope you and your children enjoy the stories and characters we present to you here.

These Fairy tales have been passed down from parent to child for generations and generations. They usually teach a lesson. They teach the values that are important in every culture; like being kind, generous and helpful to others. They show that looks can be deceiving. Something beautiful, can be cruel and evil. But something ugly, can be good and loving. They also teach the value of patience. Rewards for good deeds don't always come quickly. But be patient, and the good deeds you do will bring good deeds to you. And if you keep working hard, your efforts will pay off.

I have tried my best to re-tell these stories in modern and natural English, without being too complicated or too hard. Most middle school children can read these stories. But I hope that parents and other adults will enjoy reading these books with their children too. There are interesting parts in each story. I hope there is enough that everyone will enjoy reading the story and listening to the native speakers.

Again, thank you for joining us in Story House. We hope you enjoy your stay.

이 책을 펴내며

안녕하세요. 월드컴의 Story House에 오신 것을 환영합니다. 부디 여러분과 여러분의 자녀들이 이 책이 들려주는 이야기들을 만끽하시길 바랍니다.

이 동화들은 부모에서 아이들에게로 여러 세대에 걸쳐 전해내려 온 이야기로서 교훈을 담고 있습니다. 이웃에게 친절하고 서로 도우면서 아낌없이 베푸는 것, 이러한 가치관의 중요성을 일깨워 주죠. 이러한 것들은 때때로 반대로 표현되기도 합니다. 겉보기에는 아름답지만 잔인하고 사악할 수 있으며, 비록 흉칙하게 보여도 착하고 사랑을 베푸는 사람일 수 있다는 것입니다. 이러한 이야기들은 우리에게 인내의 가치를 일깨워 주기도 합니다. 선한 행동의 대가는 그 즉시 되돌아오지 않습니다. 그러나 참고 기다린다면, 여러분의 선한 행동은 보답을 받을 것입니다. 그리고 열심히 노력한다면 그에 상응하는 결과를 얻을 것입니다.

저는 이 이야기들을 너무 복잡하거나 어렵지 않도록 현대적이고 자연스러운 영어로 전달하기 위해 최선을 다했습니다. 이 책은 중학교 수준의 학생이라면 누구든지 읽을 수 있습니다. 그러나 부모님을 비롯한 모든 이들이 자녀분들과 함께 이 책을 즐길 수 있기를 바랍니다. 이야기마다 제각기 재미있는 부분들이 있습니다. 네이티브들이 들려주는 생생한 이야기는 현장감을 더해 주어 자신도 모르는 사이에 동화세계에 빠져들게 될 것임을 믿어 의심치 않습니다.

다시 한 번 저희 Story House에 오신 것을 감사드리며, 계속 많은 사랑 부탁드립니다.

Lori Olcott

등장인물 주요 등장 인물

오로라 공주
성장하자마자 심술궂은 마녀의 저주로 물레에 찔려 100년 동안 잠을 자게 된다.

왕자
용감하고 마음씨를 착한 왕자. 잠자는 숲 속의 미녀를 구하러 가시덩쿨로 둘러싸인 성으로 향한다.

선한 요정
오로라 공주의 세례식에 참석하여 악한 요정의 저주를 100년 간의 깊은 잠으로 바꾼 현명한 요정.

악한 요정
오로라 공주의 세례식에 초대받지 못한 데에 앙심을 품고 공주에게 죽음이라는 저주를 내린다.

그 외의 등장 인물

 왕과 왕비

요정들

 마을 사람들

전의들

Contents

Chapter 1   10
Comprehension Checkup I   28

Chapter 2   32
Comprehension Checkup II   52

Chapter 3   56
Comprehension Checkup III   76

Chapter 4   80
Comprehension Checkup IV   106

Answers   110
Word List   114

Chapter 1

Once upon a time in a far away kingdom, there was a king and queen. They were kind and good, and they ruled their kingdom well. One year, the queen was going to have a baby. When it was time for the baby to be born, the queen had a lot of trouble. Then, as the sun rose over the mountain, the baby finally came. She was a baby girl.

once upon a time 옛날 옛적에
rule 통치하다, 다스리다
be going to …할 예정이다
have a baby 아기를 낳다
be born 태어나다
trouble 고생, 수고

as …하자
rise 오르다, (해,달 등이)뜨다
mountain 산
finally 마침내
come(came-come) 태어나다

One year, the queen was going to have a baby.
어느 해, 왕비가 출산할 시기가 다가왔습니다.

as the sun rose over the mountain, the baby finally came.
해가 산 너머에 떠오르자 마침내 아기가 태어났습니다.

What a beautiful baby girl we have. Her eyes are as blue as the sky, and her hair is as yellow as the sun. What shall we name her?

Let's name her Aurora. Aurora means "dawn", the time of day when she became our daughter.

Aurora is the perfect name. Her christening will be a holiday. We will have a big feast and a dance. Everyone will be invited.

as… as~ ~처럼[만큼] …한
name 이름을 짓다
mean 의미하다
become(-became-become)
    …이 되다
perfect 완벽한, 이상적인

christening 세례식
holiday 공휴일
feast 연회, 잔치
everyone 모든 사람
invite 초대하다

Aurora means "dawn", the time of day when she became our daughter. 오로라는 '새벽'을 뜻하고 이 아이는 그 시간에 태어났으니까요.

Her christening will be a holiday.
이 아이의 세례식날을 공휴일로 정하겠소.

Everyone will be invited. 모든 이들이 초대될 것이오.

Who will be her godmother? She must have a godmother.

 We will ask all the good fairies in the kingdom to be her godmothers. She will be the luckiest princess in the world.

The king sent messengers to find all the good fairies in the kingdom and invite them to the christening. Seven good fairies answered the invitations. They all wanted to give princess Aurora special, magical gifts.

godmother 대모
ask 부탁하다, 묻다
fairy 요정
luckiest (lucky의 최상급)
  가장 운이 좋은
in the world 세상에서

send(-sent-sent) 보내다
answer 회답하다
invitation 초대, 초대장
want to …하기를 원하다
special 특별한
magical 신비한, 마법의

We will ask all the good fairies in the kingdom to be her godmothers.
왕국의 모든 선한 요정들에게 대모가 되어 달라고 부탁할 것이오.

They all wanted to give princess Aurora special, magical gifts.
요정들 모두가 오로라 공주에게 특별한 마법의 선물을 주고 싶어했습니다.

Soon, the day of the christening arrived. People from all over the kingdom showed up to eat, dance and give presents to the baby princess. Everyone had a wonderful time. The king also had some gifts to give.

Good fairies, thank you for being Aurora's godmothers. I have presents for you. Here are seven gold boxes with silver necklaces inside. I hope you like them.

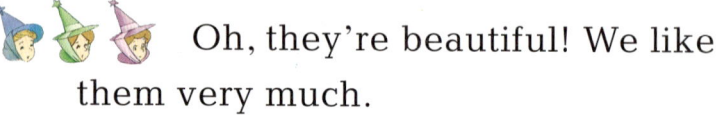 Oh, they're beautiful! We like them very much.

soon 곧, 머지않아
arrive (때가)오다
show up (구어체)
  (모임 등에)나오다, 나타나다

have a wonderful time
  즐거운 시간을 보내다
necklace 목걸이
inside …안에

Soon, the day of the christening arrived.
머지않아 세례식날이 다가왔습니다.

I have presents for you. 여러분께 드릴 선물을 준비했소.

I hope you like them. 마음에 들었으면 좋겠소.

Suddenly, an old fairy appeared.

 Where is my gold box and silver necklace?

 Who are you?

 I am also a fairy. Why didn't you invite me? Is it because I am old and ugly? Did you only invite the young, pretty fairies?

 No, fairy, we did not want to offend you. We sent out messengers to find all the fairies. They could not find you. I am so sorry. Please, sit with us and be one of my daughter's godmothers.

Is it because I am old and ugly?
내가 늙고 추하기 때문인가?

Please, sit with us and be one of my daughter's godmothers.
자, 우리와 함께 앉아서 당신도 내 딸의 대모가 되어 주오.

suddenly 갑자기
appear 나타나다
invite 초대하다
pretty 예쁜

offend 감정을 상하게 하다
send(-sent-sent) out 파견하다
messenger 전령

The old fairy sat with the others, but she was very angry.

 No invitation for me. No gold box for me. No silver necklace for me. I will teach these people a lesson. Never offend a fairy.

One of the good fairies heard the old fairy. She became afraid for the princess.

 The old fairy wants to hurt the princess. I don't know what she will do. How can I save her?

sit(-sat-sat) 앉다
teach (a person) a lesson
  혼내 주다, 교훈을 주다
never 결코[절대] …않다

hear(-heard-heard) 듣다
afraid 걱정하여, 근심하여
hurt 해를 끼치다, 상처를 입히다
save 구하다

I will teach these people a lesson. Never offend a fairy.
이 사람들에게 결코 요정을 화나게 하면 안 된다는 교훈을 일깨워 줘야겠군.

She became afraid for the princess.
그녀는 공주가 걱정되었습니다.

Then it was time for the fairies to give Aurora her magical gifts. The fairies gathered around the baby's basket. The good fairy who heard the old fairy decided to hide instead.

 I think the old fairy will give the princess an evil gift. If I give my gift last, maybe I can help her.

The good fairy who heard the old fairy decided to hide instead.
늙은 요정이 하는 소리를 들은 착한 요정은 모이는 대신 숨기로 했습니다.

If I give my gift last, maybe I can help her.
내가 마지막에 축복을 내린다면 공주님을 도울 수 있을지도 몰라.

gather around 둘러싸다, 모여들다
baby's basket 아기 요람
decide …하기로 하다, 결정하다
hide 숨다

instead 그 대신에
evil 사악한
last 마지막으로
maybe …일지도 모르다

My gift is beauty and a smile to light the land.

My gift is kindness and a gentle, loving hand.

My gift is intelligence, a strong and level mind.

My gift is music, play any tune you find.

My gift is dancing with light and graceful feet.

My gift is singing, a voice so soft and sweet.

beauty 아름다움
smile 미소
light 밝게 하다, 가벼운
kindness 친절함
gentle 부드러운
loving hand 사랑스러운 손길

intelligence 지혜
level mind 정직한 마음
play 연주하다
tune 곡조, 곡
graceful feet 우아한 발놀림

My gift is beauty and a smile to light the land.
제 선물은 아름다움과 이 나라를 비춰 줄 미소랍니다.

My gift is dancing with light and graceful feet.
제 선물은 가볍고 우아한 발놀림으로 춤추는 것이랍니다.

Finally, the old fairy stepped up to the baby princess.

> My gift is death,
> a fate both cold and sad.
>
> This is your curse for
> treating me so bad.
>
> Before you are full grown,
> a spindle sharp and true
>
> Will prick your little finger,
> and that's the end of you!

The old fairy laughed evilly and vanished in a puff of smoke.

This is your curse for treating me so bad.
이것은 나를 홀대한 대가로 네게 내리는 저주란다.

The old fairy laughed evilly and vanished in a puff of smoke.
늙은 요정은 불길한 웃음을 남기고는 연기와 함께 사라졌습니다.

finally 마침내, 드디어
step up 다가가다
death 죽음
fate 종말, 운명
curse 저주, 천벌, 재앙
treat 대접하다, 대우하다
spindle 물레가락, 방추

sharp 날카로운
prick 찌르다
laugh 웃다
vanish 사라지다
a puff of 한 모금의
smoke 연기

Comprehension

Checkup I

I True or False

1. The princess was named Aurora, because Aurora was her grandmother's name.
2. The king wanted to invite everyone to Aurora's christening.
3. The king and queen asked the fairies to be Aurora's godmothers.
4. The king gave the fairies silver hairpin.
5. The old fairy wanted to hurt the princess.

II Multiple Choice

1. **When is it dawn?**
    a. At the beginning of the day.
    b. In the middle of the day.
    c. At the end of the day.

2. **How many fairies answered the invitations to the christening?**
    a. Six fairies answered the invitations.
    b. Seven fairies answered the invitations.
    c. Eight fairies answered the invitations.

3. Why was the old fairy angry?

   a. Because she had to come to the christening.

   b. Because she didn't get an invitation.

   c. Because she didn't have a magical gift for the princess.

4. Why did one good fairy hide?

   a. Because she wanted to give her gift last.

   b. Because she didn't want to give Aurora anything.

   c. Because she was afraid of the old fairy.

5. What things did the good fairies not give Aurora?

   a. Intelligence, kindness and beauty.

   b. Singing, dancing and music.

   c. Beautiful jewelry and clothes.

Comprehension

Checkup I

III **Fill in the Blanks - use the words in the word bank**
(each word is used once)

all	blue	born	luckiest	never
showed	teach	time	world	yellow

1. When it was _____ for the baby to be _____, the queen had a lot of trouble.

2. Her eyes are as _____ as the sky, and her hair is as _____ as the sun.

3. She will be the _____ princess in the _____.

4. People from _____ over the kingdom _____ up to eat, dance and give presents.

5. I will _____ these people a lesson. _____ offend a fairy.

정답은 p.110에

IV **Draw a line to connect the first half of each sentence with the second half:**

A	B
The king and queen	was a beautiful baby girl.
The princess	gave Aurora many magical gifts.
The silver necklaces	were kind and good rulers.
The good fairies	cursed the princess.
The old fairy	were in gold boxes.

Chapter 2

The king shouted in anger, and the queen almost fainted with grief.

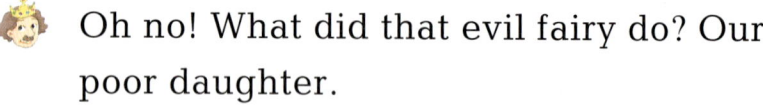
Oh no! What did that evil fairy do? Our poor daughter.

How terrible. We can't let our daughter die.

Wait! I think I can help. I have not given my gift yet.

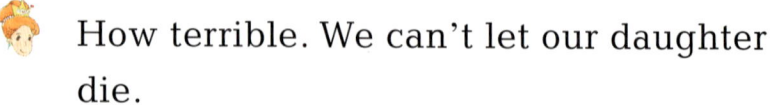
Can you take away the curse?

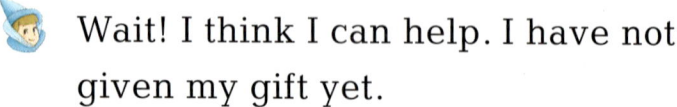
No, I can't do that. But I can change it a little.

shout in anger 화가 나서 소리치다
faint with grief 슬픔으로 실신하다
terrible 무서운, 끔찍한
let …하게 하다

give(-gave-given) 주다
away 사라져, 없어져
change 바꾸다
a little 약간, 조금

The king shouted in anger, and the queen almost fainted with grief.
임금님은 분노에 겨워 소리쳤고 왕비는 슬픔으로 거의 실신 상태가 되었습니다.

We can't let our daughter die. 우리 공주를 죽게 내버려 둘 수는 없어요.

I have not given my gift yet. 전 아직 선물을 드리지 않았어요.

My gift is hope.
Aurora will not die.

When the spindle pricks her,
deep sleep will close her eye.

Many years will come and
go until the evil's past.

A brave and kindly prince will
come and wake her up at last.

 Thank you, good fairy.
But how long will
she sleep?

 She will sleep for
a hundred years.

 A hundred years?!
Why will she sleep
for so long?

hope 희망
spindle 물레가락, 방추
deep sleep 깊은 수면
close one's eye 눈을 감다
evil 악, 악의

past 끝난, 지나간
brave 용감한
wake up 깨우다
at last 마침내
for so long 오랫동안

Many years will come and go until the evil's past.
저주가 풀리기까지 많은 세월이 흐를지니.

A brave and kindly prince will come and wake her up at last.
어느 한 용감하고 친절한 왕자가 와서 마침내 공주를 깨우리라.

There is a lot of evil in the curse. It will take a hundred years for the evil to run out.

 I don't want our daughter to sleep for a hundred years. I will prevent the curse from happening. I order that all spindles and spinning wheels in the kingdom will be destroyed. If there are no spindles, Aurora can't prick her finger. Then the curse will be prevented.

 What a wonderful idea, dear!

 Maybe it will help, but the old fairy's magic is strong. Please be careful.

I order that all spindles and spinning wheels in the kingdom will be destroyed. 짐은 이 나라 안에 있는 모든 물레가락과 물레들을 파괴할 것을 명하노라.

Maybe it will help, but the old fairy's magic is strong.
도움이 될지도 모르겠군요. 하지만 늙은 요정의 마법은 강하답니다.

take(-took-taken) (시간이)걸리다
run out 다 없어지다, 바닥나다
prevent 방지하다

order 명령하다
spinning wheel 물레
destroy 파괴하다, 없애다

And so, the king sent out his order. All over the kingdom, people gathered up all the spindles and spinning wheels they could find and burned them. It took many months, but finally, there were no more spindles in the kingdom. No one wanted the princess to prick her finger and sleep for a hundred years.

all over the kingdom
  온 왕국에서
gather up 한데 모으다
burn 불태우다

no more 더 이상 …않다
no one 아무도 …않다
for a hundred years 백 년 동안

All over the kingdom, people gathered up all the spindles and spinning wheels they could find and burned them.
왕국 도처에서 백성들은 그들이 찾아낼 수 있는 모든 물레가락과 물레들을 한데 모아 불태웠습니다.

Many years passed, and Aurora grew into a lovely young lady. All the good fairies' gifts came true. She was beautiful, kind and intelligent. She also could sing, dance and play any musical instrument easily. Everyone loved her, and she was very happy. But sometimes she got bored.

pass 지나다
grow(-grew-grown) 자라다
come(-came-come) true
 들어맞다, 실현되다
intelligent 총명한, 재치있는

musical instrument 악기
easily 손쉽게
sometimes 때때로, 이따금
get(-got-gotten) bored
 권태를 느끼다

Many years passed, and Aurora grew into a lovely young lady.
오랜 세월이 흘러 오로라는 어여쁜 젊은 숙녀로 자라났습니다.

But sometimes she got bored.
그러나 때로는 지루하기도 했습니다.

The Sleeping Beauty

I'm tired of studying, and I don't feel like playing any music now. I think I'll explore the castle. This castle is so big. I'll never see every room in it. Hey, here is a tower I've never climbed before. I wonder what is at the top.

The princess climbed up the long stairway. Higher and higher she went. Finally, she opened a door into a little room. There she saw an old woman working with a big spinning wheel.

be tired of 싫증나다
feel like …ing …하고 싶어지다
explore 탐험하다
never 일찍이 …없다
　　　한 번도 …않다
see(-saw-seen) 보다
Hey! (기쁨·놀람)어머나, 이런

climb 오르다, 등반하다
wonder …이 아닐까 생각하다
　　　알고 싶어하다
at the top 꼭대기에
stairway 계단, 층계
work 일하다

I'm tired of studying, and I don't feel like playing any music now.
공부에 싫증났고 지금은 어떤 음악도 연주하고 싶지 않아.

Hey, here is a tower I've never climbed before.
어머나, 내가 한 번도 올라가 본 적 없는 탑이 여기 있네.

Good afternoon. ma'am. What are you doing?

Well hello, princess. I am spinning thread.

Spinning thread? Why?

Where do you think cloth comes from? First you have to make thread. To make thread, you spin it.

How do you do that?

This is called a spinning wheel. I push this pedal with my foot. When I push the pedal, it makes the big wheel go around.

How interesting!

When the big wheel goes around, it makes this little part spin. That's why they call the little part the spindle.

ma'am (부인의 존칭)아주머니, 부인
spin (실을)잣다, 돌다
thread 실
come from …에서 오다[나오다]
first 우선

pedal with one's foot
 발로 페달을 밟다
go around 돌아가다, 돌다
How interesting! 정말 재밌군요!
part 부분

Where do you think cloth comes from?
공주님께서는 천이 어디서 만들어진다고 생각하시나요?

When the big wheel goes around, it makes this little part spin.
That's why they call the little part the spindle.
큰 바퀴가 돌아가면 이 조그만 부분이 돌면서 실을 만들죠. 그래서 이 조그만 부분을 물레가락이라고 부른답니다.

Wow, it spins so fast.

 Here is some wool. I put some wool on the spindle and start the big wheel. When the spindle spins, it pulls the wool and twists it tightly into thread. And that's how you make thread. When you have lots of thread, you can weave it into cloth. Then you can make new clothes.

 Amazing! I've never seen a spinning wheel before. Is it difficult?

 No, it's easy.

 May I try it?

 Of course, my dear. Here is some wool, and here is the spindle.

wool 양모
twist 감다, 꼬다
tightly 단단히, 팽팽하게
weave (천을)짜다, 뜨다
Amazing! 놀랍군요!, 굉장하군요!
May I …? …해도 될까요?

When the spindle spins, it pulls the wool and twists it tightly into thread. 물레가락이 돌아가면서 양모를 당기고 그것을 단단하게 감아서 실을 만드는 거예요.

May I try it? 제가 해 봐도 될까요?

Aurora reached for the wool and the spindle. Suddenly, the spindle slipped and pricked her little finger. Instantly, she fell to the floor. The old woman began to laugh. She was really the evil, old fairy in disguise.

 Ha, ha, ha, ha, ha! Die, princess Aurora, die! Now my revenge is complete. That will teach the king and queen a lesson. They'll never forget me again.

The old fairy vanished in a puff of smoke.

She was really the evil, old fairy in disguise.
그녀는 사실 노파로 변장한 사악하고 늙은 요정이었습니다.

Now my revenge is complete. 이제 내 복수는 이루어졌도다.

instantly 즉시, 즉석에서
revenge 복수
complete 완성된, 끝난

teach (a person) a lesson
  혼내 주다, 교훈을 주다
vanish 사라지다

Fortunately, a servant was passing by and found the princess.

 Your highness, are you all right? Princess, wake up. Why won't you wake up? Why is this spinning wheel here? Oh no, it's the evil fairy's curse. Help, help! The princess is under a curse!

Fortunately, a servant was passing by and found the princess.
다행히도 한 신하가 그곳을 지나가다가 공주를 발견했습니다.

Why won't you wake up? Why is this spinning wheel here?
왜 깨어나시지 못하세요? 왜 이 물레가 여기 있는 거지?

fortunately 다행히(도)
pass by 옆을 지나가다
all right 건강한, 무사한

wake up 일어나세요
be under a curse 저주받다

Comprehension
Checkup II

I **True or False**

1. The good fairy could not take away the curse.
2. The fairy said that Aurora would fall asleep, but never wake up.
3. Many people hid their spindles and did not burn them.
4. Aurora saw an old woman sewing clothes.
5. Aurora pricked her finger on the spindle.

II **Multiple Choice**

1. Why will Aurora sleep for a hundred years?
   a. Because the good fairy's magic was not strong.
   b. Because it would take that long for the evil to run out.
   c. Because she will be very, very tired.

2. Where do you usually find spindles?
   a. They are usually with spinning wheels.
   b. They are usually on the dining table.
   c. They are usually in gold boxes.

The Sleeping Beauty

정답은 p.111에

3. Why did the king order that all spindles would be destroyed?

   a. Because he didn't like spindles.

   b. Because he wanted to make the old fairy happy.

   c. Because he wanted to prevent the curse from happening.

4. What did Aurora find when she explored the castle?

   a. She found a secret door behind a curtain.

   b. She found a tower she had never climbed before.

   c. She found a garden she had never seen before.

5. What did Aurora think about spinning thread?

   a. She thought it was too difficult.

   b. She thought it was boring.

   c. She thought it was interesting.

Comprehension
Checkup II

III **Fill in the Blanks - use the words in the word bank**
(each word is used once)

anger	dance	fainted	have	in
musical	passing	princess	really	spin

1. The king shouted in _____, and the queen almost _____ with grief.

2. She could sing, _____ and play any _____ instrument easily.

3. First you _____ to make thread. To make thread, you _____ it.

4. She was _____ the evil, old fairy _____ disguise.

5. Fortunately, a servant was _____ by and found the _____.

The Sleeping Beauty

IV **Draw a line to connect the first half of each sentence with the second half:**

A	B
When you push the spinning wheel pedal,	it pulls the wool and twists it into thread.
When the wheel goes around,	you can make new clothes.
When the spindle spins,	it makes the spindle spin.
When you have lots of thread,	it makes the wheel go around.
When you have lots of cloth,	you can weave it into cloth.

Chapter 3

The servants carried Aurora to her bedroom. The king called the royal doctors. They pinched her arms, patted her face, rubbed her head with water and gave her medicine. But nothing helped. The princess did not wake up.

royal doctor 궁중 전의
pinch 꼬집다
pat 가볍게 두드리다
rub 문지르다

They pinched her arms, patted her face, rubbed her head with water and gave her medicine. 그들은 그녀의 팔을 꼬집고 뺨을 가볍게 두드려 보기도 하고 머리를 물로 문지르고 투약도 해 봤습니다.

But nothing helped. 그러나 아무 소용이 없었습니다.

I'm sorry, but there is nothing else we can do. She is not sick. This is fairy magic.

Oh, our poor daughter.

We need to call the good fairy.

Suddenly, the good fairy appeared.

You don't need to call me. I am here. A little bird told me what happened.

Thank you for coming here.

else 그 밖의, 다른
sick 병든
don't need to …할 필요가 없다

what happened
어떤 일이 있었는지

I'm sorry, but there is nothing else we can do.
죄송합니다만 저희들이 할 수 있는 것은 이 밖에 아무것도 없습니다.

A little bird told me what happened.
조그만 새가 무슨 일이 있었는지 말해 주었답니다.

Is Aurora in pain?

No, she is not in pain. She is sleeping peacefully. Now I must complete my spell. A hundred years will pass before she wakes up. Many things will change over the years. When she wakes up, she will need something familiar. Therefore, some people will also sleep for a hundred years. Then she will not be lonely in her new world.

Many things will change over the years.
그 세월 동안 많은 것이 변할 것입니다.

When she wakes up, she will need something familiar. Therefore, some people will also sleep for a hundred years.
그녀가 깨어나면 낯설지 않은 무언가를 필요로 할 것입니다. 그러니 몇몇 사람들도 (오로라 공주와 함께) 백 년 동안 잠을 자야 합니다.

be in pain 아파하다
be ···ing ···하고 있다
peacefully 평온하게
complete 완성하다, 끝마치다

familiar 낯익은, 익숙한
therefore 그러므로
lonely 고독한, 쓸쓸한

 We will sleep too.

 No, you must rule the country. I cannot put the whole kingdom to sleep. Let us ask everyone in the castle. Some people must sleep to help the princess, but others must stay awake to help you.

The good fairy asked everyone in the castle who wanted to sleep for a hundred years. Everyone said they wanted to help the princess. But the good fairy insisted that some people stay awake to help the king and queen.

Some people must sleep to help the princess, but others must stay awake to help you. 몇몇 사람들은 공주님을 돕기 위해 잠을 자야 하지만 그 외의 사람들은 폐하를 돕기 위해 깨어 있어야 합니다.

The good fairy asked everyone in the castle who wanted to sleep for a hundred years. 착한 요정은 성 안의 모든 사람들에게 누가 공주와 함께 백 년 동안 잠을 자고 싶은지 물어 봤습니다.

rule 통치하다, 다스리다
stay awake 깨어 있다

ask 묻다
insist 주장하다

Finally, she chose a hundred ladies, gentlemen and servants to sleep.

Everyone else must leave the castle now. When I cast my spell, everyone inside the castle will fall asleep for a hundred years.

The king, the queen and the rest of their ladies, gentlemen and servants left the castle to rule the kingdom.

choose(-chose-chosen)
  뽑다, 선택하다
leave 떠나다
cast one's spell 주문을 걸다

fall asleep 깊은 잠을 자다
rest 나머지
servant 신하, 하인

When I cast my spell, everyone inside the castle will fall asleep for a hundred years. 제가 주문을 걸면 성 안에 있는 모든 사람들은 백 년 동안 잠을 자게 될 것입니다.

After they were gone, the good fairy cast her spell.

> Sleep, sleep, sleep well all.
> Into deepest sleep you'll fall.
> Sleeping for a hundred years
> Until a royal son appears.

One by one, the ladies, gentlemen and servants in the castle fell asleep. Soon, there were no sounds but the singing of birds and the snoring of the people inside.

Sleep, sleep, sleep well all. 잠들라, 잠들라, 모두 고이 잠들라.
Into deepest sleep you'll fall. 모두가 깊은 잠에 빠져 들지니라.
Sleeping for a hundred years 백 년 동안의 깊은 잠 속으로
Until a royal son appears. 고귀한 왕자가 나타날 때까지.

be gone 떠나다
one by one 한 사람씩, 차례로
soon 곧, 금새

no sound 아무 소리도 안 나다
snore 코골다

Just then, the old fairy returned.

 So, you think you can save Aurora from my curse? Never. She might wake up, but no one will ever find her. I will keep everyone away.

> Grow, grow briar and thorn,
> Never broken, never torn.
>
> Keep all visitors away!
> In her castle, she will stay.

---

return 돌아오다	keep away 가까이 못하게 하다
never 결코[절대] …않다	briar 찔레
no one 아무도 …않다	thorn 가시
ever (부정문에서)결코, 전혀	tear(-tore-torn) 찢다, 째다

Grow, grow briar and thorn, 자라거라, 자라거라, 찔레꽃과 가시여.
Never broken, never torn. 절대 부러지지도 말고 결코 찢기지도 마라.
Keep all visitors away! 모든 방문객들을 들이지 말지니.
In her castle, she will stay. 공주는 성에만 머물 것이로다.

The old fairy waved her hands, and briars and thorns began to grow all around the castle. Soon, the castle was covered in thick vines with long, sharp thorns. Anyone who tried to enter the castle would get scratched and badly hurt.

 So there! Now no one will ever come here. The princess will be forgotten and lost.

wave 흔들다, 휘두르다
cover 뒤덮다
thick vine 울창한 덩굴
sharp 날카로운, 예리한

get scratch 긁히다
be badly hurt 심하게 다치다
forget(-forgot-forgotten) 잊다
lose(-lost-lost) 죽다, 사라지다

Anyone who tried to enter the castle would get scratched and badly hurt. 성 안에 들어가려는 사람은 누구든지 긁히고 심한 상처를 입게 될 것입니다.

The princess will be forgotten and lost.
공주는 잊혀지게 되어 결국은 죽음을 맞이할 것이다.

No. If there is life, there is hope. I will make sure that people remember the beautiful princess inside the castle.

> Grow, grow flower and leaf,
> Beauty in the dark of grief.
> Showing all that hope remains
> For any who will brave the pains.

The good fairy waved her hands, and beautiful flowers grew between the dangerous thorns.

Now people will see the beautiful flowers, and they will remember the princess who is waiting for her prince.

Grow, grow flower and leaf, 자라거라, 자라거라, 꽃과 잎사귀여
Beauty in the dark of grief. 슬픔의 어둠 속에 있는 미녀여.
Showing all that hope remains 남은 모든 희망을 보여 주어라
For any who will brave the pains. 고난과 용감히 맞설 이를 위하여.

life 생명
hope 희망
make sure 확신하다
leaf 잎사귀
grief 슬픔, 비탄

remain 남아 있다
brave 용감히 맞서다
pain 고통, 아픔
dangerous 위험한

We'll see. A hundred years is a long time. They will all forget.

 Yes, we'll see. A hundred years is a long time. But some will remember.

And so time passed. The king and queen grew old and died. People came and went through the kingdom. Towns grew into cities, and some cities shrank into towns. Wars were fought, and peace was restored. Time made its changes across the land.

grow old 늙다
come and go 지나가다
war 전쟁
fight(-fought-fought) 싸우다

peace 평화
restore 복구하다, 회복시키다
across the land 온 나라에

People came and went through the kingdom.
사람들이 왕국을 거쳐 갔습니다.

Wars were fought, and peace was restored. Time made its changes across the land.   여러 번의 전쟁을 거친 후 평화가 찾아왔습니다. 세월이 온 나라를 변화시켰습니다.

Comprehension

Checkup III

I True or False

1. The royal doctors could not wake up the princess.
2. The king and queen wanted to sleep for a hundred years too.
3. Everyone in the castle wanted to stay awake to help the king and queen.
4. The old fairy wanted everyone to remember the sleeping princess.
5. A hundred years is a long time.

II Multiple Choice

1. What was wrong with the princess?
   a. She was sick.
   b. She was dead.
   c. She was under fairy magic.

2. How did the good fairy know that Aurora was under the curse?
   a. A little bird told her.
   b. The king sent a messenger.
   c. She saw through a magic mirror.

3. **Why did the fairy want other people to sleep for a hundred years also?**

   a. To make the evil curse run out faster.

   b. So that the princess would not be lonely when she woke up.

   c. Because the fairy was really the old fairy in disguise.

4. **How would the briars and thorns keep people away from the castle?**

   a. They were sharp and dangerous.

   b. They smelled very bad.

   c. They made the castle hard to find.

5. **What happened to the king and queen?**

   a. They slept for a hundred years.

   b. They forgot about Aurora.

   c. They grew old and died.

Comprehension
Checkup III

III **Fill in the Blanks - use the words in the word bank**
(each word is used once)

| change | cities | else | from | hope |
| life | shrank | sorry | think | years |

1. I'm _____, but there is nothing _____ we can do.

2. Many things will _____ over the _____.

3. So, you _____ you can save Aurora _____ my curse?

4. If there is _____, there is _____.

5. Towns grew into _____, and some cities _____ into towns.

정답은 p.112에

IV Draw a line to connect the first half of each sentence with the second half:

A	B
When Aurora wakes up,	briars and thorns grew around the castle.
When I cast my spell,	she will need something familiar.
When the king and queen were gone,	they will remember the princess.
When the old fairy waved her hands,	the good fairy cast her sleep spell.
When people see the beautiful flowers,	everyone in the castle will fall asleep.

Chapter 4

Finally, a hundred years passed. A new family ruled the kingdom. The prince of the new royal family was a strong and handsome young man. His favorite sport was horseback riding, and he loved to ride for miles and miles around.

pass (때가)지나다, 경과하다
a royal family 왕실, 왕가
favorite 가장 좋아하는

horseback riding 승마
love 매우 좋아하다

His favorite sport was horseback riding, and he loved to ride for miles and miles around. 그가 가장 좋아하는 운동은 승마였고 먼 곳까지 말을 타고 여행하는 것을 좋아했습니다.

One day, he noticed an old castle up on a hill. The castle was covered in vines. It looked like no one had lived there for a long time. He rode to the town nearby to ask about it.

Excuse me. Does anyone live in the castle up on the hill?

The castle up on the hill? Evil witches live there. That is why it is covered with briars and thorns. They want to keep people away.

notice 알아차리다
for a long time 오랫동안
ride(-rode-ridden) to
  …로 말을 타고 가다

nearby 가까이에, 근처에
anyone 누군가
evil witch 사악한 마녀

Does anyone live in the castle up on the hill?
누군가 언덕 위에 있는 저 성에 살고 있나요?

That is why it is covered with briars and thorns.
그래서 찔레꽃과 가시들로 덮여 있는 것이지요.

Witches? No, not witches. The castle is cursed by evil monsters. If you go there, they will eat your eyes and your heart.

What are you talking about? Everyone knows that the castle is filled with evil witches. Many people have gone there, but no one ever returns.

That is because the ghosts ate their eyes and hearts.

curse 저주하다   fill with …으로 가득차다
monster 괴물   ghost 유령

Many people have gone there, but no one ever returns.
많은 사람들이 저곳에 갔지만 아무도 돌아오지 않았답니다.

That is because the ghosts ate their eyes and hearts.
그건 유령들이 그들의 눈과 심장을 먹어 버렸기 때문이죠.

The Sleeping Beauty

You're both wrong. A sleeping princess waits for her prince inside the castle.

 What? A sleeping princess?

 Yes, sir. My great-grandfather worked in the castle long ago. He told the story of the sleeping princess to my grandfather. My grandfather told the story to my father. And my father told the story to me.

 What is this story?

both 둘 다, 양쪽 모두
wrong 틀린, 잘못된
wait for …을 기다리다

great-grandfather 증조부
work 일하다

A sleeping princess waits for her prince inside the castle.
성 안에는 잠자는 공주가 왕자님을 기다리고 있어요.

What is this story? 그 이야기란 어떤 것인가요?

Long ago, a king, a queen and their beautiful daughter lived there. One day, they accidentally offended a powerful fairy. The fairy put a curse on the princess. The evil fairy wanted the princess to die. Fortunately, a good fairy helped her. Instead of dying, the princess fell asleep for a hundred years. Only a brave and kind prince can save her. But few princes are truly brave and kind.

accidentally 뜻하지 않게
offend 감정을 상하게 하다
put a curse on
　…에게 저주를 내리다

fortunately 다행히(도)
instead of …대신에
truly 진정으로

Instead of dying, the princess fell asleep for a hundred years.
죽는 것 대신에 그 공주님은 백년 동안 잠을 자게 되었습니다.

But few princes are truly brave and kind.
하지만 진정으로 용감하고 친절한 왕자는 드물지요.

The Sleeping Beauty

Well, many people tell me I am kind. I will try to save her.

 But sir, many young men have gone to find her, but no one ever came back.

 Then I must be brave. Don't worry. I'll be careful. Thank you for your help.

The prince rode off to the castle. Soon, he came to the wall of thorns and briars.

save 구하다　　　　　　　　　　ride off 말을 타고 떠나다
careful 조심하는, 주의하는　　　　wall 벽

But sir, many young men have gone to find her, but no one ever came back.　하지만 왕자님, 많은 젊은이들이 공주님을 찾으러 갔지만 여태까지 돌아온 사람은 아무도 없습니다.

These thorns look sharp. I must be careful. But the flowers here are so beautiful. Maybe there really is a beautiful princess inside. I will pick a flower for her. She'll like that.

The prince carefully reached between the thorns and picked a flower. Suddenly, a magical path appeared between the thorns.

 Amazing! Now I can get to the castle easily.

sharp 날카로운
reach (손 등을)뻗다, 내밀다
magical path 마법의 통로

Amazing! 놀랍군!, 굉장하군!
easily 쉽게

These thorns look sharp. I must be careful.
이 가시들은 날카로워 보이는군. 조심해야겠어.

The prince carefully reached between the thorns and picked a flower.
왕자는 조심스럽게 가시덤불 사이로 손을 뻗어 꽃 한 송이를 꺾었습니다.

The prince started to walk to the castle. As he walked, the path closed behind him.

Oh, no! I can't get out. Maybe this is the monsters' trap. Oh well, I must be brave. I'll go on.

Finally, he came to the castle door. The door opened easily, and the prince went into the courtyard. There, he saw many people fast asleep.

as …하자
close 닫히다
get out 나가다
trap 함정, 속임수

go on 나아가다, 계속하다
finally 마침내, 드디어
courtyard 안뜰, 앞마당
fast asleep 깊이 잠들다

As he walked, the path closed behind him.
그가 걸어가고 있자니 뒤에서 통로가 닫혀 버렸습니다.

Oh well, I must be brave. I'll go on.
그건 그렇고, 난 용감해져야 해. 계속 가야지.

How strange? Who are all these people? They don't look like witches or monsters. Their clothes are from a hundred years ago. They are all asleep, just like the story of the princess. Maybe it's true. Maybe there really is a sleeping beauty here. I wonder where she is.

The prince searched all through the castle.

how (감탄문에서) 참으로, 얼마나
strange 이상한
look like …인 것 같다

just 꼭, 바로
wonder …인가하고 생각하다
all through 내내, 줄곧

How strange? Who are all these people?
정말 이상하군! 이 사람들은 모두 누굴까?

I wonder where she is.   공주는 어디 있는 걸까?

Finally, he found Aurora's bedroom. She was still as beautiful as she was a hundred years ago. And she was still sleeping peacefully.

Amazing! I can't believe she has been asleep for a hundred years. She looks so young and beautiful. Well princess, I don't know how to wake you, but I brought you a flower. I hope you like it.

The prince put the flower in Aurora's hand.

She was still as beautiful as she was a hundred years ago.
그녀는 백 년 전과 마찬가지로 여전히 아름다웠습니다.

Well princess, I don't know how to wake you, but I brought you a flower. I hope you like it. 그런데 공주, 당신을 어떻게 깨워야 할지 모르겠소만 당신을 위해 꽃을 가져왔소. 마음에 들었으면 좋겠구료.

still 여전히
as… as~ ~처럼[만큼] …한
peacefully 평온하게

bring(-brought-brought) 가져오다
put 두다, 놓다

Suddenly, her eyes opened, and she woke up.

Hello. What happened? Where am I?

I don't know. I heard a story that you were asleep for a hundred years.

Asleep for a hundred years? Oh, no! The curse!

At that moment, the good fairy appeared.

Yes, princess Aurora. You were asleep for a hundred years. Remember when you pricked your finger on a spindle? That is when you fell under the evil curse. Then this young prince saved you.

remember 기억하다
prick 찌르다
spindle 물레가락, 방추

fall under the curse
저주에 걸리다

What happened? Where am I?
무슨 일이 있었던 거죠? 여긴 어딘가요?

That is when you fell under the evil curse.
그 때가 바로 공주님께서 사악한 저주를 받았을 때랍니다.

I did? How did I save her?

 You were brave to come to the castle and walk through the wall of briars. And you were kind to bring the princess a flower. Most princes only think about themselves. You think of others. That is a great kindness. Now, I must wake up everyone else.

> Wake, wake, wake up all!
> Rise and hear your lady's call.
> All is well beneath this roof.
> True love's smiles will be the proof.

Wake, wake, wake up all! 깨어나라, 깨어나라, 모두 깨어나라!
Rise and hear your lady's call. 일어나서 공주님의 부르심을 받들라.
All is well beneath this roof. 이 성의 지붕 아래 모든 이가 무사하도다.
True love's smiles will be the proof.
진정한 사랑의 미소가 그 증거가 될지니.

rise 일어서다
hear 듣다
call 부르는 소리, 요구

beneath …의 바로 밑에
proof 증거, 입증

And it was true. The prince and the princess were in love.

 I'm so glad you came for me. Thank you for saving me.

 I'm glad I could help you. I love you. Will you marry me?

 Of course! I love you too.

And so the prince and princess were married. All the ladies, gentlemen and servants from Aurora's castle went with her to the prince's castle. And they all lived happily ever after.

I'm so glad you came for me. Thank you for saving me.
절 위해 와 주셔서 정말 기뻐요. 그리고 구해 주셔서 감사드립니다.

All the ladies, gentlemen and servants from Aurora's castle went with her to the prince's castle.
오로라 공주의 성에 있던 모든 신사숙녀와 신하들은 공주와 함께 왕자님의 성으로 갔습니다.

be in love 사랑하다
Thank you for …ing
　…해 주어 감사하다
glad 기쁜
be married 결혼하다
ever after 이후 내내

Comprehension

Checkup IV

I. True or False

1. Everyone in the town knew who lived in the castle.
2. Only a brave and kind prince can save the sleeping princess.
3. It was difficult for the prince to follow the path through the thorns.
4. Aurora was still sleeping peacefully after a hundred years.
5. The prince and the good fairy fell in love.

II. Multiple Choice

1. Why did the townsperson know about the sleeping princess?
   a. His father told him the story.
   b. He read about it in a book.
   c. He saw her in the castle.

2. Why did the prince pick a flower?
   a. He wanted to put the flower in his hat.
   b. He wanted to give the flower to his mother.
   c. He wanted to give the flower to the princess.

정답은 p.113에

3. **What happened when the prince picked the flower?**

   a. A path appeared between the thorns.

   b. The thorns all disappeared.

   c. The flower died and turned brown.

4. **Who appeared when Aurora woke up?**

   a. The king and queen appeared.

   b. The evil, old fairy appeared.

   c. The good fairy appeared.

5. **What great kindness did the prince show?**

   a. He killed the old fairy.

   b. He thought of others instead of himself.

   c. He picked flowers for all the sleeping people.

Comprehension

Checkup IV

III **Fill in the Blanks - use the words in the word bank**
(each word is used once)

asleep	believe	eat	eyes	hundred
like	long	story	there	woke

1. It looked _____ no one had lived there for a _____ time.

2. If you go _____, they will _____ your eyes and your heart.

3. They are all _____, just like the _____ of the princess.

4. I can't _____ she has been asleep for a _____ years.

5. Suddenly, her _____ opened, and she _____ up.

정답은 p.113에

IV Draw a line to connect the words that are opposites of each other:

A	B
Shrink	Forget
Begin	Peace
War	Last
First	Complete
Remember	Grow

Comprehension Checkup

Checkup I (28~31p)

I 1. F   2. T   3. T   4. F   5. T

II 1. a   2. b   3. b   4. a   5. c

III 1. time, born   2. blue, yellow
3. luckiest, world   4. all, showed
5. teach, never

IV

A	B
The king and queen	was a beautiful baby girl.
The princess	gave Aurora many magical gifts.
The silver necklaces	were kind and good rulers.
The good fairies	cursed the princess.
The old fairy	were in gold boxes.

Matches:
- The king and queen — were kind and good rulers.
- The princess — was a beautiful baby girl.
- The silver necklaces — were in gold boxes.
- The good fairies — gave Aurora many magical gifts.
- The old fairy — cursed the princess.

Comprehension Checkup

Checkup II (52~55p)

I 1. T   2. F   3. F   4. F   5. T

II 1. b   2. a   3. c   4. b   5. c

III 1. anger, fainted   2. dance, musical
3. have, spin   4. really, in
5. passing, princess

IV

A	**B**
When you push the spinning wheel pedal,	it pulls the wool and twists it into thread.
When the wheel goes around,	you can make new clothes.
When the spindle spins,	it makes the spindle spin.
When you have lots of thread,	it makes the wheel go around.
When you have lots of cloth,	you can weave it into cloth.

Comprehension Checkup

Checkup III (76~79p)

I 1. T   2. T   3. F   4. F   5. T

II 1. c   2. a   3. b   4. a   5. c

III
1. sorry, else
2. change, years
3. think, from
4. life, hope
5. cities, shrank

IV

A	B
When Aurora wakes up,	briars and thorns grew around the castle.
When I cast my spell,	she will need something familiar.
When the king and queen were gone,	they will remember the princess.
When the old fairy waved her hands,	the good fairy cast her sleep spell.
When people see the beautiful flowers,	everyone in the castle will fall asleep.

Matches:
- When Aurora wakes up → she will need something familiar.
- When I cast my spell → everyone in the castle will fall asleep.
- When the king and queen were gone → briars and thorns grew around the castle.
- When the old fairy waved her hands → the good fairy cast her sleep spell.
- When people see the beautiful flowers → they will remember the princess.

The Sleeping Beauty

Comprehension Checkup

Checkup IV (106~109p)

I 1. F   2. T   3. F   4. T   5. F

II 1. a   2. c   3. a   4. c   5. b

III
1. like, long
2. there, eat
3. asleep, story
4. believe, hundred
5. eyes, woke

IV

A	B
Shrink	Forget
Begin	Peace
War	Last
First	Complete
Remember	Grow

- Shrink — Grow
- Begin — Last
- War — Peace
- First — Complete
- Remember — Forget

다음은 이 책에 나오는 단어와 숙어를 수록한 것입니다.
＊표는 중학교 영어 교육 과정의 기본 어휘입니다.

A

a little	33
a puff of	27
a royal family	81
accidentally	88
across the land	75
afraid*	21
all over the kingdom	39
all right	51
all through	97
Amazing!	47 / 93
answer*	15
anyone	83
appear*	19
arrive*	17
as*	11 / 94
ask*	15 / 63
as ··· as ~	13 / 99
at last	35
at the top	43
away*	33

B

baby's basket	23
be ···ing	61
be badly hurt	71
be born	11
be going to	11
be gone	67
be in love	105
be in pain	61
be married	105
be tired of	43
be under a curse	51
beauty*	25
become*	13
beneath	103
both*	87
brave	35 / 73
briar	68
bring*	99
burn*	39

114 The Sleeping Beauty

C

call*	103
careful	91
cast one's spell	65
change*	33
choose*	65
christening	13
climb*	43
close*	94
close one's eye	35
come*	11 / 40
come and go	75
come from	45
complete*	49 / 61
courtyard	94
cover*	71
curse	27 / 84

D

dangerous*	73
death	27
decide*	23
deep sleep	35
destroy	37

E

easily	40 / 93
else*	58
ever*	68
ever after	105
everyone	13
evil	23 / 35
evil witch	83
explore	43

F

faint with grief	33
fairy	15
fall asleep	65
fall under the curse	101
familiar	61
fast asleep	94
fate	27
favorite	81
feast	13
feel like doing	43
fight*	75
fill with	84
finally*	11 / 27 / 94
first*	45
forget*	71

for a hundred years	39	have a wonderful time	17
for a long time	83	hear*	21 / 103
for so long	35	Hey!	43
fortunately	51 / 88	hide*	23
		holiday*	13
		hope*	35 / 73
		horseback riding	81

G

gather around	23	how*	97
gather up	39	How interesting!	45
gentle	25	hurt*	21
get bored	40		
get out	94		

I

get scratch	71	in the world	15
ghost	84	inside*	17
give*	33	insist	63
glad*	105	instantly	49
go around	45	instead*	23
go on	94	instead of	88
godmother	15	intelligence	25
graceful feet	25	intelligent	40
great-grandfather	87	invitation	15
grief	73	invite*	13 / 19
grow*	40		
grow old	75		

H

J

have a baby	11	just*	97

116 The Sleeping Beauty

K

keep away	68
kindness	25

L

last	23
laugh*	27
leaf*	73
leave*	65
let*	33
level mind	25
life*	73
light*	25
lonely*	61
look like	97
lose*	71
love*	81
loving hand	25
luckiest	15

M

ma'am	45
magical	15
magical path	93
make sure	73

May I …?	47
maybe*	23
mean*	13
messenger	19
monster	84
mountain*	11
musical instrument	40

N

name*	13
nearby	83
necklace	17
need to	58
never*	21 / 43 / 68
no more	39
no one	39 / 68
no sound	67
notice*	83

O

offend	19 / 88
once upon a time	11
one by one	67
order*	37

P

pain*	73
part*	45
pass*	40 / 81
pass by	51
past*	35
pat	57
peace*	75
peacefully	61 / 99
pedal with one's foot	45
perfect	13
pinch	57
play*	25
pretty*	19
prevent	37
prick	27 / 101
proof	103
put*	99
put a curse on	88

R

reach*	93
remain	73
remember*	101
rest*	65
restore	75
return*	68
revenge	49
ride off	91
ride to	83
rise*	11 / 103
royal doctor	57
rub	57
rule*	11 / 63
run out	37

S

save*	21 / 91
see*	43
send*	15 / 19
servant	65
sharp	27 / 71 / 93
shout in anger	33
show up	17
sick*	58
sit*	21
smile*	25
smoke*	27
snore	67
sometimes	40
soon*	17 / 67
special*	15
spin	45

The Sleeping Beauty

spindle	27 / 35 / 101
spinning wheel	37
stairway	43
stay awake	63
step up	27
still*	99
strange*	97
suddenly	19

T

take*	37
teach (a person) a lesson	21 / 49
tear	68
terrible	33
Thank you for ···ing	105
therefore*	61
thick vine	71
thorn	68
thread	45
tightly	47
trap	94
treat	27
trouble*	11
truly	88
tune	25
twist	47

V

vanish	27 / 49

W

wait for	87
wake up	35 / 51
wall*	91
want to	15
war*	75
wave	71
weave	47
what happened	58
wonder*	43 / 97
wool	47
work*	43
work in	87
wrong*	87

THE SLEEPING BEAUTY
19 잠자는 숲 속의 미녀

펴낸이 | 강 남 현
펴낸곳 | 월드컴출판사
주소 | 서울시 구로구 구로동 222-8 (우편번호 152-848)
코오롱 디지탈타워 빌란트Ⅱ 1005호
전화 | 02)3273-4300(대표)
팩스 | 02)3273-4303
이메일 | wc4300@yahoo.co.kr
홈페이지 | www.wcbooks.co.kr

* 본 교재는 저작권법에 의해 보호를 받는 저작물이므로
무단전재 및 무단복제를 금합니다.